Échappé (eh-sha-PAY) on pointe

One   Two   Three

Tallulah's Toe Shoes

by **MARILYN SINGER**

Illustrations by
ALEXANDRA BOIGER

CLARION BOOKS
Houghton Mifflin Harcourt | Boston | New York

Thanks to Steve Aronson, Laurie Shayler, and the ballet students
at Third Street Music School, as well as my wonderful editor,
Jennifer Greene, and the good folks at Clarion/HMH Books. —M.S.

Clarion Books
215 Park Avenue South, New York, New York 10003

Clarion Books is an imprint of Houghton Mifflin Harcourt Publishing Company.
www.hmhbooks.com

The text was set in Pastonchi MT Std.
The illustrations were executed in watercolor, as well as watercolor mixed
with gouache and egg yolk, on Fabriano watercolor paper.

Library of Congress Cataloging-in-Publication Data
Singer, Marilyn.
Tallulah's toe shoes / by Marilyn Singer ; illustrated by Alexandra Boiger.
p. cm.
Summary: Tallulah is frustrated because the grownups will not let her try
dancing in toe shoes yet, so she sneaks a pair out of the wastebasket
and tries to do it on her own.
ISBN 978-0-547-48223-1 (hardcover)
1. Ballet dancing—Juvenile fiction. 2. Ballet slippers—Juvenile fiction.
[1. Ballet dancing—Fiction. 2. Ballet slippers—Fiction.]
I. Boiger, Alexandra, ill. II. Title.
PZ7.S6172Tak 2013
813.54—dc23
2012010869

Manufactured in China
SCP 10 9 8 7 6 5 4 3 2 1
4500387520

To an extraordinary teacher, mentor, and friend, Cara Gargano
—M.S.

To Paola, Camillo, and Francesco, con affetto
—A.B.

TALLULAH could stand like a ballerina. Tallulah could move like a ballerina, too. But Tallulah knew she'd never *be* a ballerina until she got a pair of pink satin toe shoes.

Ever since her ballet school's performance of
Sleeping Beauty, that was all she could think about.
Some of the older girls at the school danced
on pointe—up on their toes in pointe shoes.

One of them got to be the beautiful Lilac
Fairy. She wore a glittery tutu and a tiara.

Tallulah was a village girl. She wore a short brown
dress and carried a hoop of fake flowers. She didn't get
to dance on her toes. She got to sway.

"When can I get toe shoes?" she asked her mother
right after the performance.

"When you're a little older," her mother replied.

That's not fair,

Tallulah huffed silently.
The kids in tap class
get their fancy shoes
right away!

School of ...

Then one day in class, her teacher said, "Tallulah, what excellent feet! You're going to be wonderful on pointe someday."

"*When is* someday?" Tallulah asked.

"When your feet are ready—when they've stopped growing," her teacher said.

But my feet ARE ready, Tallulah thought.

After class, she stomped into the dressing room. The older girls were there, tying on their pointe shoes. The Lilac Fairy was one of them.

"Well, these are wrecked," she said, studying her shoes.
"Good thing I brought a new pair." With a thud, she tossed the old ones into the wastebasket.

Tallulah's mouth made an O. She put her clothes on over her leotard and tights very, very slowly.

Soon she was the only one left in the room. She darted over to the wastebasket and stared at the shoes. They didn't look wrecked. They looked splendid. **I'll show everyone just how ready I am,** Tallulah told herself. **I will be the youngest dancer ever to dance on pointe.**

Snatching the shoes,
she stuffed them in her
bag and ran out the door.

At home, she ran straight to her room. She hugged the toe shoes, then leaned over to put them on. But which was the right and which was the left? She couldn't tell.

Eeny, meeny, miny, mo . . . left, right, she decided, and slipped into the shoes. They were a little big. She took them off again and stuffed some tissues inside. That's better, she thought.

Then she crisscrossed the ribbons
on her ankles, just the way the real
ballerinas did, and tied them in two
neat bows.

They looked *perfect!*

"Relevé, Tallulah!" she said out loud. She rose on her toes—and promptly plopped to the floor.

Pulling herself up by her chair, she tried again—

and fell down again.

She held on to the doorknob and tried once more.
Biting her lip, she bent her knees to get on her toes.
That made it easier. But when she looked in the
mirror, she didn't look much like the Lilac Fairy.
She looked more like a rat.

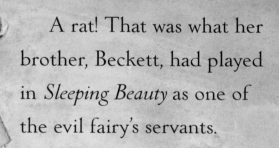

A rat! That was what her brother, Beckett, had played in *Sleeping Beauty* as one of the evil fairy's servants.

Then suddenly she remembered—the Lilac Fairy
had danced with the handsome prince. Tallulah didn't
have a handsome prince, but she did have a brother—
and he even took ballet!

"Wow! Where did you get those?"
Beckett asked when he saw her shoes.
"Never mind that now. I need
you to be the prince."
"Uh, okay," he said.

Tallulah gave him her hand
and rose up on her toes. Her knees
buckled. "Stand up taller!"
she commanded.

"I'm standing as tall as I can!"
he replied.

Tallulah sighed. "Get on the chair,"
she said.

Beckett did. This time when he took
her hand, Tallulah stayed on pointe.

I'm a princess, and
I'm dancing on my toes!
she thought. But her toes were
beginning to hurt.

"Now I'm going to move in
a circle," Tallulah said. "Hold
on tight!"

I'm the
Lilac Fairy,
and I'm turning
on my toes!
Tallulah thought.

But her toes hurt even worse.

"Can we stop now?" Beckett asked.
"This is boring."

"Boring? Don't you
want to be the prince
someday?"

"I'd rather be a rat.
It was a lot more fun,"
Beckett said.

He scurried around the room, doing his ratty steps. "Or maybe a cat—Puss-in-Boots!"

"Then go away! A real ballerina doesn't need RATS or CATS in her room!" Tallulah commanded, standing on her toes once more.

Beckett shrugged and scurried out.

As soon as he was gone, Tallulah sank to the floor. "Ow!"
she moaned. "Ow, ow, ow!" She pulled off the shoes. Her toes
were hot and red.

I can't do it.
I can't dance on pointe.
She whimpered.
I'll never be the princess
or the Lilac Fairy.
Never ever.

All week Tallulah was sad, but she didn't tell anyone why.

After her next ballet class, she waited again in the dressing room till everyone had gone. She took the toe shoes out of her dance bag and looked at them with a sigh. Then she tossed them into the wastebasket.

At that very moment, the Lilac Fairy came back into the room.
She raised an eyebrow at Tallulah, walked over to the basket,
and looked inside. "Are those my old pointe shoes?"

Tallulah lowered her eyes.

"Did you take them home?"

Still not looking at the older girl,
Tallulah blushed and nodded.

For a moment, the Lilac Fairy was silent. Then she said, "Did your toes hurt when you put them on?" This time, Tallulah did look up. The girl was trying not to smile.

"And did you stand like this?" She bent over just the way Tallulah had. She looked like a rat, too. A big one.

"Yes," Tallulah whispered.

This time, the girl did smile. "I never thought I'd get my own pointe shoes and learn to dance on my toes. But I did."

She rose beautifully on pointe and did several quick little steps
back and forth.

Just then, Beckett stuck his head in the door. "Tallulah! Come and
watch! We're learning fifth position!" He hurried back to class.

"That's my brother," Tallulah explained. "He was a rat in the *Sleeping
Beauty* ballet. He's going to be Puss-in-Boots in that ballet someday."

"He probably will be," said the girl. She grabbed a towel from her cubby.

"And someday I'm going to be the Lilac Fairy," Tallulah announced.

"Maybe. If you're good enough and you work really hard." The girl patted her hair, which was in a bun, and waved goodbye over her shoulder.

Tallulah looked down at the toe shoes in the basket. "Not someday *maybe*—someday *definitely*," she said.

Then, patting her hair, which was still just a little too short
to put in a bun, she leaped across the room to join her brother.

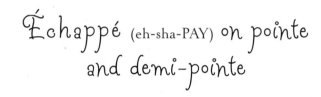

Échappé (eh-sha-PAY) on pointe
and demi-pointe

One

Tw